KEY HUNTERS

THE WIZARD'S WAR

KEY HUNTERS

*Getting lost in a good book
has never been this dangerous!*

THE MYSTERIOUS MOONSTONE

THE SPY'S SECRET

THE HAUNTED HOWL

THE WIZARD'S WAR

KEY HUNTERS

THE WIZARD'S WAR

by Eric Luper

Illustrated by Lisa K. Weber

SCHOLASTIC INC.

> *To Julia, who has helped keep*
>
> *me on course*

Text copyright © 2017 by Eric Luper.
Illustrations by Lisa K. Weber, copyright © 2017 Scholastic Inc.

All rights reserved. Published by Scholastic Inc., *Publishers since 1920.* SCHOLASTIC, SCHOLASTIC PRESS, and associated logos are trademarks and/or registered trademarks of Scholastic Inc.

This book is being published simultaneously in hardcover by Scholastic Press.

The publisher does not have any control over and does not assume any responsibility for author or third-party websites or their content.

Library of Congress Cataloging-in-Publication Data

Names: Luper, Eric, author. | Weber, Lisa K., illustrator. | Luper, Eric. Key hunters ; #4.
Title: The wizard's war / by Eric Luper ; illustrated by Lisa K. Weber.
Description: New York, NY : Scholastic Inc., 2017. | Series: Key hunters ; #4
Summary: This time Cleo, Evan, and Ms. Crowley (who, it turns out, is the missing Ms. Hilliard's sister) find themselves in a confusing fantasy book, caught up in a war with wizards, elves, trolls, and the mighty Golden Dragon—and while they manage to find their missing librarian, their quest does not end there.
Identifiers: LCCN 2016030471| ISBN 978-0-545-82214-5 (hardcover) | ISBN 978-0-545-82213-8 (paperback)
Subjects: LCSH: Books and reading—Juvenile fiction. | Libraries—Juvenile fiction. | Magic—Juvenile fiction. | Librarians—Juvenile fiction. | Locks and keys—Juvenile fiction. | Detective and mystery stories. | Adventure stories. | CYAC: Mystery and detective stories. | Books and reading—Fiction. | Libraries—Fiction. | Magic—Fiction. | Locks and keys—Fiction. | Adventure and adventurers—Fiction. | GSAFD: Mystery fiction. | Adventure fiction. | LCGFT: Detective and mystery fiction. | Action and adventure fiction.
Classification: LCC PZ7.L979135 Wi 2017 | DDC 813.6 [Fic] —dc23
LC record available at https://lccn.loc.gov/2016030471

10 9 8 7 6 5 4   17 18 19 20 21

Printed in the U.S.A.   40
First printing 2017

Book design by Mary Claire Cruz

CHAPTER 1

"Are you both ready?"

Their librarian, Ms. Crowley, wore her usual pointy, clicky high heels, but everything else about her outfit was out of the ordinary. She was wearing a pink vest and a curly tail. On her face, she wore a rubber pig nose.

"Ready for what?" Cleo asked, looking around their school library. "To huff and puff and blow a house down?"

Ms. Crowley blushed and pulled off the

costume. "First graders pay attention better when I dress up during read-aloud."

Evan and Cleo followed Ms. Crowley to the darkest corner of the library. It felt strange to trust the woman who had stood in their way on their last three adventures. But they had the same goal—to find their old librarian, Ms. Hilliard, who had mysteriously disappeared into one of the magical books in the secret library beneath their school. For Ms. Crowley, the stakes were higher. Ms. Hilliard was her sister.

Ms. Crowley reached up and tugged on a huge, dusty, boring-looking book titled *Literature: Elements and Genre from Antiquity to Modern-Day.*

The bookcase swung open to reveal a dark stairway.

When they reached the bottom, the fireplace at the rear of the hidden library poofed to life. Evan looked around. It was the same as he remembered. Shelves, sliding ladders, and spiral staircases stretched into the darkness above them. Catwalks and balconies reached around corners and across gaps to let readers explore every nook. Above the fireplace hung a tapestry that showed an image of an open book with people swirling into it among a sea of colorful letters.

Cleo held up the brass key they had gotten on their last adventure. "How do we know which book this unlocks?"

"With enough searching, you can find anything in a library," Ms. Crowley said. She led them up a spiral staircase and across a narrow bridge.

"Watch your heads," she said, ducking into a dark passageway. They crossed to another catwalk, slid down a brass pole, and wound behind a maze of shelves. Hanging oil lamps lit their way.

At the end of an aisle stood a pedestal that held a thick book. The cover was made of reptile skin and was fastened shut by a large chain and a lock. The title read: *The Dragon's Eye.*

"Does that heavy chain mean . . ." Evan trailed off.

Ms. Crowley nodded. "Whatever is hiding inside this book is pretty dangerous."

Evan looked worried. "Do we have to unlock it?"

"We do if we want to find my sister," Ms. Crowley said.

"Then what are we waiting for?" Cleo slid the key into the lock and twisted.

The book popped open. Letters burst from the pages like a thousand crazy spiders. The letters tumbled in the air around them and began to spell words. The words turned into sentences, the sentences paragraphs. Before long, they could barely see through the letter confetti. Then everything went black.

CHAPTER 2

Evan and Cleo found themselves in the grand hall of a run-down castle. Light streamed through tall windows. Torn tapestries hung from the walls. Chairs and tables lay broken in pieces. Ms. Crowley was nowhere to be seen. As they looked around, a serious voice broke the silence.

"My name is Vixa," a girl said.

Evan and Cleo spun to face her. She wore a red cloak over a suit of armor. A sword hung from her belt and a silver headband with a glowing red gem circled her head. "I am aide to Tannis, adviser to King Ledipus, ruler of the Kingdom of Bissel. We need your help. Follow me."

"I'm already confused," Cleo said. She wore a leather vest with metal studs and soft boots. Her ears were pointy at the tops.

"You're an elf!" Evan said.

Cleo felt her ears. "I'm a confused elf," she said. "King who? Aide to what?"

"Fantasy books can be confusing," Evan whispered. He wore blue robes decorated with gold stars and moons, and a pointed hat that flopped over. A leather pouch hung from his belt. "Sometimes the strange names are enough to make me want to stop reading. Just stick with it."

"It's not like we have a choice," Cleo said. "Hey, where's Ms. Crowley?"

"She must be somewhere else in the book."

Evan dug through his pouch. Small vials lined the bag. Several scrolls were stuffed alongside them. He figured he must be a wizard.

"Wizard. Rogue," Vixa called, already halfway down the hall. "Follow me. Time is short."

"I'm a rogue?" Cleo asked.

"Of course you're a rogue," Evan said. "Look at your outfit."

"Sweet," Cleo said. "What's a rogue?"

"It's like a thief and an acrobat mixed together."

"Double sweet!"

They followed Vixa to a dark chamber. A

withered man wearing a crown slumped on a throne. A hooded man crouched at his side. Vixa looked at the king with concern.

"Good, you've come," the hooded man said. "The king has an important matter to discuss with you." He whispered in the king's ear. The king's mouth quivered. A tiny moan rattled out.

"His majesty has fallen ill," the man said. "I am Tannis, the king's trusted adviser. I will help him tell you what we need."

"What's the trouble?" Cleo said.

"You rogues are all alike," Tannis said. "Always getting right to business."

"Well, most of these books have a problem that needs to be solved," Cleo said.

"Most of these whats?" Tannis asked.

"She means the *world* has many problems that need solving," Evan said.

"Very true." Tannis circled to the other side of the throne and put his ear to the king's mouth. "The king would like you to make peace with the wood elves. Vixa will be your guide."

"What's the trouble with the wood elves?" Evan asked.

"They have waged war against us."

Vixa placed her hand on her sword. "The elves feel we have taken their land. They attack our traders as punishment."

"Well, did you?" Evan asked.

"Did we what?" Tannis said.

"Did you take their land?"

"We cut down a few trees," Tannis said. "The wood elves think all forests belong to them. And their allies, the dwarves, try to claim our underground mines as their own. That's why we've had to bring in the trolls to

oversee their work. The Kingdom of Bissel needs resources to prosper. We cannot be distracted by jealous creatures."

"I'm more confused than ever," Cleo whispered.

Evan hushed her.

"This war needs to end," Vixa said, "especially with rumor of the Golden Dragon awakening."

"The Golden Dragon?" Evan asked.

"Have you never heard of the Golden Dragon?" Vixa looked shocked. "It's the most fearsome beast the land has ever seen. Larger than a mountain. Fiery breath that can melt solid stone."

"Standing together, there is a chance we may defeat the dragon," Tannis said. "If we remain divided, we are all doomed."

"Doomed is bad," Cleo said.

"We must travel across the plains, through a mountain pass, and into the dark forest," Vixa said.

Cleo brightened. "That seems okay."

"The journey will be filled with foul beasts," Tannis added.

"Ew," Evan said.

"This should be a simple matter for a clever rogue and a powerful wizard," Vixa said. The glowing gem on her headband dimmed for a moment and she blinked her eyes.

Tannis waved his hand and the gem glowed brightly again.

"You must meet with the queen of the wood elves," Tannis said. "Offer her peace if she will join us. It is the only way we'll defeat the Golden Dragon and save both our kingdoms."

The king moaned and Tannis murmured in his ear. "Now, go," Tannis said. "There's no time to lose."

Evan wanted to help. Clearly, this kingdom *needed* help. But something didn't feel right.

"What's in it for us?" Cleo asked.

"What are you doing?" Evan whispered.

"If I'm a rogue, I should act like one."

"Spoken like a true scoundrel," Tannis said. He held out a silver goblet. It was filled with gemstones of all colors. "Make peace with the elves and you can have as much treasure as you can carry."

Cleo sunk her hand into the fancy cup. As the gems trickled through her fingers, her eyes widened. "I've got big hands."

"Vixa has prepared your horses," Tannis said. "Once you have the queen's promise, use this." He handed Vixa a shimmering cube. "It's a magic crystal. Smash it and it will return you here. Bring me good news."

The king moaned again. His crown slipped down his forehead.

"Bring *us* good news," Tannis corrected himself. "Return peace to the Kingdom of Bissel. Return honor to the throne of King Ledipus."

Vixa bowed, turned, and marched from the throne room. Evan and Cleo did the same.

As Vixa silently led them out of the castle gates toward the stables, Cleo turned a cartwheel.

"Being a rogue is kind of nice," she said. "I feel stronger and faster."

"I wish *I* felt different," Evan said.

"What do you mean?"

Evan patted his pocket and pulled out a slender wand. The handle was wrapped in braided leather. He swished the tip of his wand through the air. Green sparks crackled out.

"I have no idea how to use this thing," he said. "If I have to cast a spell, I think we're in trouble."

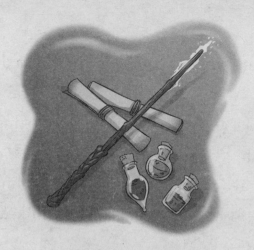

CHAPTER 3

They'd been riding for a few hours when Evan noticed something was wrong with Cleo. He turned his horse to face her. "What's the matter?" he asked.

Cleo's eyes were clenched shut. "Horses make me nervous."

Evan thought back on the fun two weeks he'd spent at Camp White Pine, where he rode every morning. "Haven't you ever ridden?"

"Once, at my cousin's birthday party."

"See, you're practically a pro," Evan said, following Vixa down a grassy slope.

Cleo pushed herself up, but immediately buried her face in her horse's mane. "Daisy the donkey bucked me off," Cleo complained. "And she pooped a lot."

Evan worried that Cleo might not be able to keep up, but he also felt a little proud that for once he was better at something than she was.

They followed Vixa through fields of grass that swayed in the breeze. They crossed a river and headed into the mountains. Red cliffs rose around them until they reached a ridge where they could see for miles in every direction. It was hard to believe that nasty creatures could live in a land this beautiful.

Finally, they came upon a dark cave hidden by mist. Bones lay in piles around the entrance. The stench of rotting meat hung in the air.

The horses began to fidget and twitch.

Something flew past Evan's face and struck a tree behind him. He turned to see a thick spike sticking out of the wood.

"Who dares approach my lair?" a deep voice snarled.

Vixa dismounted her horse. Evan and Cleo did the same. The horses whinnied and backed away.

"We mean you no harm," Vixa said.

"Then why is your hand on your sword?" the voice asked.

Evan peered into the darkness of the cave. Two glowing eyes peered back. He heard a low growl.

Moments later, a massive creature crept out. At first, Evan thought it was a lion. As it stepped into the light, he realized it was something much stranger. This lion had giant bat wings, and the end of its tail was covered in sharp spikes.

The gem on Vixa's headband glowed brightly. She lifted her sword and charged.

The creature flicked its tail. Two spikes flew at Vixa. One knocked her sword from her hand. The other pinned her cloak to the ground.

"You mean me no harm?" the creature countered.

"Foul beast!" Vixa cried, tugging on her cloak.

"I know a fouler one," the creature said. It turned to Evan and Cleo. "My name is Darius. I am a manticore. I come from lands to the East."

"Looks like you live right here." Cleo

poked her boot at a bone lying on the ground. "Looks like you *eat* right here, too."

"Everyone must eat," Darius said. "As for living here, I'm afraid I have a problem."

"What sort of problem?" Evan asked warily.

"Don't speak to him," Vixa warned. "The vile words of the manticore will twist your thoughts."

"Pay her no mind." Darius spread his wings, revealing a torn section on his right side. "Trolls attacked me, and manticore wings do not heal," he said. "I'm stuck here, away from my family, away from my kingdom."

"You're a king?" Evan asked.

"Don't listen to him," Vixa warned. "Manticores lie."

Darius ignored Vixa. "A prince, actually. And general of the manticore army. But here, I'm nothing more than an animal hunting for my next meal." He lifted his tail. "I suppose you three will do."

"You have to let us pass," Cleo said. "We're on a mission for King Ledipus."

"Save your breath," Darius said. "Meat gets tough if the creature is worried."

Vixa pulled her cloak free of the spike. "It is said that a manticore must let us pass if we can answer its riddle."

"Oh, not that old tradition." Darius sighed.

"Yes, a riddle," Evan said.

"Oh, very well," Darius said. "Answer my riddle and I will let you pass."

"All three of us?" Cleo said.

"All three of you."

"Good, a three-for-one deal," Cleo muttered. "I hate riddles."

Darius paced back and forth in front of

his cave as he thought. "If I keep it, I don't share it. If I share it, I destroy it. What am I?"

"Um, anything?" Cleo said. "Keeping things means you don't share them. This is a dumb riddle. Give us another one."

"No," Darius said. "I'll take worried meat over no meat at all."

"We should have attacked when we had the chance," Vixa said.

"We can solve this," Evan said. "The first part is hard. 'If I keep it, I don't share it.' That could be anything. But the second part is different. 'If I share it, I destroy it.' What's destroyed if you share it?"

"A lollipop?" Cleo said. "If someone licks my lollipop, I throw it away. Gross."

"It's not a lollipop," Evan said.

"It's really not so bad being my lunch," Darius said. His tongue flicked out of his mouth. "Think of it as part of nature's circle of life."

"What is this, *The Lion King*?" Cleo said.

"A secret!" Evan blurted out. "The answer to your riddle is a secret!"

"Of course it's a secret," Cleo said. "If he told us the answer, it wouldn't be a riddle!"

"No, the answer to the riddle—'If I share it, I destroy it'—it's 'a secret'!"

Darius sagged a little. "I really hate this tradition," he said. "But you are correct, little ones. Go past safely."

Cleo peered along the mountain trail. It looked narrow and led to a dark forest. "Is it safe?"

Darius chuckled. "Not at all," he said. "A little manticore like me should be the least of your worries. The forest is not nearly as kind as I am."

CHAPTER 4

The mountain pass wound along cliffs so narrow Evan thought the horses might fall. Cleo whimpered behind him, but he figured it was best to leave her alone. Anyhow, the horses seemed to know where to step.

Mountains soon gave way to easier ground. They rode across grassy hills until they came to the forest. Trees grew so thick that the edge of the woods looked like a high wall. Before it, a field of stumps poked from the ground.

"Is this what Tannis calls *a few trees*?" she said. "It must be hundreds!"

"Thousands," Evan said.

"That's a small price to pay for the glory of the kingdom." Vixa led them into the forest. "It is said that the elves can sense when anyone enters their woods. They're like spiders trapping their prey in a giant web."

"I'm an elf," Cleo said. "I can't feel this forest at all."

"That's because you're a moon elf, not a forest elf," Vixa said. "Don't you know what you are?"

"I'm, uh . . . I was raised by, uh, giraffes on the Plains of Cleodonia," Cleo stammered.

Vixa looked puzzled but turned to the trail.

"Raised by giraffes?" Evan whispered to Cleo. "Good story."

"I had to think of something."

They rode on until their horses began stomping nervously.

"We must go on by foot," Vixa said, dismounting. Her horse spun around and trotted out of the forest.

Evan and Cleo dismounted, too. As their horses galloped away, Evan could tell they sensed something he couldn't.

The forest was dark as night. Vines hung low across the trail, and the clicking and chirping of bugs surrounded them.

"Creepy," Cleo said.

"Giraffe girls aren't used to the forest." Evan chuckled.

"Hush." Vixa drew her sword with her free hand. "Something isn't right."

"Yeah, we're walking straight into this weird forest," Cleo said.

The bugs stopped clicking and chirping. The silence was creepier than the noise had been.

"What is it?" Evan whispered.

Vixa peered through a clump of bushes. "Trolls."

Two creatures dressed in rags fumbled over each other in a clearing. Their skin was lumpy and green like pea soup. One had a full head of hair and the other was bald on top with a ring of stringy hair around the sides. Even from this distance, Evan could smell them.

"Sweaty feet," Cleo whispered.

"Where they are, Groo?" the one with more hair said.

"Me don't know, Grim," the bald one said. "They not far."

"If they lost, Lord Tannis will punish you."

"You are leader," Groo said. "He punish you!"

"I punish you worse!" Grim barked.

Groo grumbled under his breath.

Vixa backed away. "They were sent to watch us."

"That doesn't sound like something a kind leader would do," Evan said.

Vixa's headband glowed. "Tannis has the kingdom's best interests in mind."

"Well, I've got my nose's best interest in mind," Cleo said, "and it's away from those trolls."

Grim's head jerked in their direction. "Who there?" he growled.

Evan, Cleo, and Vixa ran away along a winding trail that led deeper into the forest. Strange, glowing moss hung around them, lighting their path. The trees were taller, and

they could see up into the branches. The treetops began to rustle. Dozens of nimble creatures swung into view above them. The creatures' angry hoots and hollers filled the air.

"What are they?" Cleo cried out.

"No idea," Evan said.

That's when the net fell on them. They were trapped!

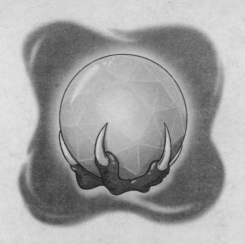

CHAPTER 5

They struggled but it was no use. Even Vixa's blade couldn't cut the net.

Evan twisted around. "We're on a mission for peace—"

"Silence, spies," a voice said. A group of elves scampered down the trees quicker than squirrels. They were dressed in patchworks of leather and cloth, and had smooth, silvery skin. "The queen will decide what to do with you."

The elves tied up Evan, Cleo, and Vixa and led them to a platform made of logs. Several elves turned a huge wooden crank. Vines pulled and the platform rose into the trees like an open-air elevator. As they rose higher, Evan saw dozens of huts built into the largest branches.

"It's just like the tree house I drew for art class," Cleo said.

"Don't waste time admiring the woodwork," Evan said. "Figure out how we can escape."

But as they neared the top, even Evan couldn't help staring in awe.

Each branch held a small building that was connected to the others by a web of bridges crisscrossing in every direction. The wood was carved with fancy designs and words in a language Evan had never seen.

At the center, in the branches of the largest tree, sat a palace made of colorful glass that glowed like a sunset.

"The queen is harsh and merciless," Vixa whispered.

"You'd have to be to survive in this forest," Cleo said.

Inside, the palace was even more beautiful. The tree trunk rose through its floor and grew out its ceiling. The walls seemed to glow on their own, lighting a large throne made of branches that reached from the tree itself. A robed woman, shadows hiding her face, stood beside the throne. A football-sized yellow diamond decorated with silver dragon claws sat on a pedestal in front of her.

"Untie them," the woman ordered.

The wood elves quickly untied Evan, Cleo, and Vixa. They rubbed their wrists.

"We found them prowling in the western woods," one of the elves said. "More spies from Bissel."

The woman stepped into the light. "Nonsense. They are no threat to us."

"Ms. Hilliard!" Evan cried out.

The woman stood tall as she paced around the kids. "I am Queen Hilliara, High Sorceress and Mistress of the Woods."

Evan looked closely. Her skin glittered and her ears were pointy like every other wood elf he'd seen, but there was no mistaking it. This was his Ms. Hilliard. He'd recognize her sparkling eyes anywhere. She winked at him.

Evan and Cleo smiled at each other. They'd finally found Ms. Hilliard, but they both knew they would have to keep her secret. Staying in character was important.

"What brings you to my palace?" Queen Hilliara asked.

"The Kingdom of Bissel wants to make peace," Cleo said.

"There will be no peace until the evil Tannis is gone," the queen said. "He has enchanted King Ledipus."

"Tannis is evil?" Evan asked, turning to Vixa.

The gem on Vixa's headband glowed brighter than ever. "Tannis knows best. He will lead his army across these lands."

"That sounds pretty evil," Evan said.

"All we need is the Dragon's Orb and our plan will be complete!"

Vixa pulled the crystal Tannis had given them from her cloak and smashed it on the floor. A magical doorway appeared. Vixa grabbed the yellow diamond from the pedestal and dove through. A blue flash blinded them for a moment, and then the doorway vanished. Vixa was gone.

"I knew she was evil," Cleo said. "She never smiled, and she always looked at me funny."

"I look at you funny and I'm not evil," Evan said.

"No, you just look funny," Cleo said.

Queen Hilliara began pacing. "What could Tannis want with the Dragon's Orb?" she wondered.

"What does it do?" Cleo asked.

"The orb has the power to control dragons, but there hasn't been a dragon in this world for a thousand years."

"Where did they go?" Cleo asked.

"They sleep deep below the earth atop mountains of treasure."

Cleo frowned. That description sounded very familiar. "Tannis offered us *handfuls* of gems," she said.

"And he seemed very interested in the underground mines," Evan added.

"The mines?" the queen repeated. "He couldn't have found—"

Just then, a wood elf rushed in. "Your Highness, an earthquake just shook the City of Bissel. We felt it in the roots of the oldest trees."

The queen stepped to the window and looked out. "It is just as I feared."

Evan and Cleo went to either side of her. "What is?" Evan asked.

"Tannis ordered the trolls to search the mines. They have been forcing the dwarves to work day and night. He must have found the Golden Dragon. With the dragon under his control, Tannis will be unstoppable!"

"So Tannis doesn't want to defeat the Golden Dragon," Cleo worked out. "He wants to use it to rule over everyone in this whole world."

"Not cool," said Evan.

Ms. Hilliard blew a silver whistle that hung from her neck. Almost immediately, a hawk landed on the windowsill.

"Sound the alarm," she told the hawk. "Call every creature on foot or wing. If we are to stop Tannis, we'll need all the help we can get."

"How can *we* help?" Evan asked Ms. Hilliard.

"I can't put my two favorite students at risk."

"I'm one of your favorite students?" Cleo asked brightly.

Ms. Hilliard smiled. "Sometimes a librarian likes a challenge."

Evan grabbed Ms. Hilliard's sleeve. "We *have* to help," he whispered. "We're the main characters in this book. We've got to face the challenge."

"It's too dangerous," Ms. Hilliard said. "Your parents can't afford to lose you."

"Our parents are a bajillion miles away," Cleo said. "If we don't save this world, we'll never find the key we need."

"No key means no way home," Evan said. He made the face he used whenever he tried to convince his mom to let him stay up late. "Ms. Hilliard, please . . ."

"Okay," she finally said. "But first you'll need some help."

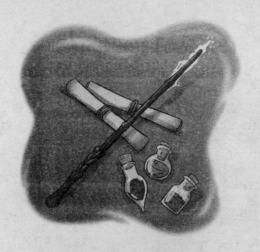

CHAPTER 6

Ms. Hilliard gave a small bottle to Cleo. It was filled with silver liquid. "This potion will heal any injury. Use it wisely. It can only be used once."

"What about me?" Evan asked. "I'm pretty sure I'm going to need more help than Cleo."

Ms. Hilliard smiled warmly. "Don't underestimate yourself," she said, handing him a velvet pouch.

Evan opened it and pulled out a pair of glasses.

"You're joking, right?" Evan said.

"Put them on," Ms. Hilliard said.

Evan put on the glasses and gasped. He could see more clearly than ever. Edges were sharper. Colors were more vivid. He looked off the balcony.

"It's poetry," he said.

"What's poetry?" Cleo asked.

"The words on the buildings. I can read it all."

"They're Spectacles of Understanding," Ms. Hilliard said. "They help you see the world better. Now, take them off and keep them safe. You can only use them for short periods of time."

"Or what?" Evan asked.

"Or they'll scramble your brains. Let's go."

"This is not how I imagined my first unicorn ride!" Cleo clenched her eyes shut as the three galloped through the forest on the backs of Ms. Hilliard's one-horned stallions.

"You've imagined yourself riding a unicorn?" Evan said.

"Every day since I was four," Cleo said. "But in my mind they had rainbow manes and glittering coats. These unicorns are muscular and sweaty and smell like piles of wet leaves."

"Watch who you call sweaty," Ms. Hilliard said. "Unicorns can be sensitive."

Cleo felt the one under her buck. "Don't

get touchy!" she whispered. "I didn't mean anything by it."

When they reached the edge of the forest, they looked out across the valley. The wood elves had already started to gather, and other creatures were joining them: woolly elephants with ten-foot tusks, bears who stood on their hind legs, a group of tiny gnomes honing their tiny swords, several centaurs, and a few circling wolves. The City of Bissel stood in the distance, smoke rising from its foundries.

"If the Golden Dragon is released, we have no hope," Ms. Hilliard said. She snapped around and started barking orders to the wood elves as more of them scampered from the trees.

"Vixa said the breath of the Golden Dragon could melt stone," Cleo said.

"Then the earthquake means—" Evan started.

Ms. Hilliard interrupted him. "It wasn't an earthquake. It was an explosion deep in the underground mines. It means Tannis is closer than we thought."

"We have to stop him," Evan said.

Another rumble shook the valley. The ground cracked, and black smoke poured out. The unicorns whinnied.

"You must get to the mines and stop Tannis, Vixa, and the trolls from releasing the Golden Dragon," Ms. Hilliard said. "But even if you make it in time, it will take many years for this world to heal."

"Heal . . . That gives me an idea," Cleo said. She sprung down from her unicorn and darted off.

Evan chased after her. "Cleo, where are you going?"

"You must hurry!" Ms. Hilliard called. But her words were lost as the two friends raced away.

Evan knew Cleo's ideas usually involved something dangerous, and he didn't really want to follow her. But what choice did he have? If he did nothing, the Golden Dragon would be released and this whole world would be doomed.

Evan ran as fast as he could, but his robes kept tripping him up. Plus, Cleo could flip and jump better than he could. After all, she was an acrobat. He was just a bumbling wizard who didn't know any spells.

Before long, Cleo was out of sight, and he was gasping for air. But when Evan looked up, he saw where Cleo was headed.

He began up the trail that led to the mountain pass.

By the time Evan reached the manticore's cave, Darius had already pinned Cleo's shoulders to the ground.

"Stop!" Cleo said. "The fate of the kingdom—"

"Manticores are not interested in human affairs."

"But the world you live in—"

"Hush now," Darius said. "I can't pass up a meal twice in one day."

Evan limped into the clearing, still out of breath. He bent over and put his hands on his knees. "What if . . . we stump *you* . . . with a riddle?" he panted.

"No one challenges *me* with a riddle."

"There's always a first time . . . for everything . . ." Evan said.

Darius took his paws off Cleo, and she scrambled away.

"I know every riddle that's ever been written," Darius said.

"No one knows *every* riddle," Cleo said.

Darius chuckled. "Try me."

Evan paced around the clearing, carefully avoiding the bones. He knew if he failed, their bones might join the pile.

"Okay," Evan said. "Here goes.

> *"Over the mountains, past a cave,*
> *Throughout the land I roam.*
> *But after all my traveling*
> *There's no place like . . . what?"*

Darius flicked his tail back and forth. "That's easy," he said as he stalked to the edge of the cliff and gazed to the East. A tear rolled down his furry cheek. "The answer is home," he whispered.

"That's right," Evan said. "What if we could get you home to your family?"

Darius flexed his torn wing. "Nonsense," he said. "Manticore wings do not heal."

Cleo took out the bottle Queen Hilliara had given her. "If we heal your wing, you have to promise to bring us to the mines of Bissel."

"A one-way trip to your doom," Darius said.

"We'll take that risk," Evan said. "How badly do you want to get home?"

Darius thought it over and offered his wing. "A manticore's word is his bond."

Cleo uncorked the bottle. "Does he drink it, or do we rub it on?" she asked.

"Let's try both."

Cleo poured some of the silvery liquid onto Darius's wing. The leathery skin began to mend. She took the rest of the potion and poured it into Darius's mouth. His rough lion tongue lapped up every drop. The manticore seemed to swell with strength. His eyes burned orange as he snapped his wings back and forth.

"Stronger than ever," he said. "I can't thank you enough."

"Now you must keep your word," Evan said.

"A one-way trip to your doom," Darius said. "Hop on."

Evan climbed onto the manticore's back and held out a hand to Cleo.

"Not another animal ride," Cleo moaned.

"Who are you calling an animal?" Darius said, offended.

"What would you rather be called?" Cleo asked as she climbed up.

He puffed out his chest. "I am Darius, Prince of the Kingdom to the East, Heir to the Throne of the Golden Mane, Lord of Riddles, Defender of Manticores, Savior of the Winged Lion Cub, Spike Hurler Extraordinaire—"

Cleo cleared her throat. "Darius, we need to get to Bissel sometime this month."

He smiled warmly. "With pleasure."

The manticore leaped off the mountain ledge and flapped his massive wings. They flew into the air and headed straight toward their doom.

CHAPTER 7

By the time they soared over the fields of Bissel, Tannis's armies were already pouring from the castle gates. Thousands of trolls with lumpy pea-green skin and stringy hair lined up to march.

"Where did that army come from?" Evan asked.

"It seems Tannis has been planning this for some time," Darius said. "Trolls never organize on their own."

Cleo buried her face in Darius's mane and whimpered.

"What's the matter?" Evan asked her.

"I don't like feeling out of control," Cleo admitted.

"I bet I know who holds the TV remote in *your* house," Evan said.

A volley of arrows hissed past them.

"They've spotted us!" Darius said. "We must fly higher."

Darius pumped his wings. They crossed over the walls of the city, swooping between the castle towers and under arching bridges.

"The mine!" Evan pointed to a tunnel where rows of small-but-stout bearded men pulled carts filled with gems. A few slimy-looking trolls stood behind them, barking orders.

"I can't believe their mothers let them out of the house like that," Cleo said.

"Maybe trolls think *we're* gross because we're so clean," Evan said.

"Speak for yourself," Cleo said. "When this adventure is over, I'm going to need a hot bath."

"*If* we get done with this adventure," Evan said. "Look . . ."

A group of trolls turned a wooden machine toward them. One of the creatures lowered his torch to the machine, and another cut a rope. A huge arm swung forward, flinging a fiery lump at them.

"Catapult!" Darius yelled. "Hang on!"

He folded his wings against his sides and twisted in the air. Evan clutched Darius's mane. Cleo screamed. The fireball roared past them. Evan could feel the heat from it as it singed Darius's fur.

Darius flicked his tail. The trolls ran for cover as manticore spikes pounded into the ground around the catapult. Darius puffed out his wings, dove, and flew straight into the mineshaft.

It took a second for their eyes to adjust.

The mine was huge. Fat wooden beams held up the ceiling, and two sets of rails ran along the floor. Rows of dwarves pulled carts from the depths of the mines. Darius soared past them to perch on a high ledge.

"This is as far as I go," he said. "It's not safe for me to fly in here."

Evan and Cleo climbed from Darius's back. Cleo looked like she was ready to kiss the ground.

"Thank you," she said. "You've been a great help."

"Are you sure you don't want to stay and fight?" Evan asked. "Queen Hilliara could really use someone like you."

"My kingdom lies far away, well out of reach of this war."

"We need to stand together," Evan said. "If Tannis defeats the wood elves, it won't be long until they conquer the manticores."

"I will seek out the trolls who injured me when I can," Darius said. "Manticores do not forgive easily. Now I must go."

Darius put a paw forward and bowed. Then he leaped from the ledge and flew out of the mine into the sunlight.

"Nice guy," Evan said.

"Nice guy?" Cleo said. "He tried to eat us!"

"He gave us a riddle and a ride to the mines."

"Evan . . . He. Tried. To. Eat. Us!"

60

They started down the largest tunnel.

"How far down do you figure this dragon is?" Cleo asked.

"I've read that some mines are more than two and a half miles deep."

The ground rumbled. Small stones and dust shook from the walls.

"We'll never make it in time," Evan said. "Tannis must be close to freeing the dragon."

"I have an idea," Cleo said. "What's the quickest way from point A to point B?"

"A straight line?" Evan asked.

"Nope." Cleo pointed to one of the unused carts resting on a track. "A runaway mine cart."

"You've got to be kidding."

"The world is about to be destroyed by an army of slimy trolls," Cleo said. "Do you have a better idea?"

Evan climbed into the cart and squatted down.

Cleo pushed it until it lurched forward and she was running to keep up. She sprang into the air, did a half-twist, and landed next to Evan.

"Ouch!" Someone was in the cart with them.

"Aaah!" Evan and Cleo screamed.

"Aaah!" the creature screamed back. "Don't hurt me!"

The dwarf was little—smaller than Evan. A dark beard draped over his round belly, and dust covered his cheeks. He wore a tiny helmet that slipped down his forehead every time he moved.

"Who are you?" Cleo asked.

"My name is Devlin, and I'm just a kid. You wouldn't hurt a kid, would you?"

"You have a beard," Evan said.

"All dwarves have beards: men, women, *and* children. And I think the question you should be asking is 'who's controlling the hand brake?' Go too fast on these tracks and we'll fly right off."

Just then, the cart shot around a curve. The two wheels on the right side lifted into the air and slammed back down on the tracks.

Cleo grabbed the hand brake and pulled it.

"Don't go too slow, either," Devlin said.

"Why?" Evan asked.

Devlin pointed behind them.

Two trolls were following in another cart. And they held big clubs.

"That's not the welcoming committee?" Evan asked.

They whipped around another curve and shot down a steep hill. The shaft opened into

a huge cave. Ahead of them, the track split into three and crisscrossed in different directions.

"We need to get to the deepest part of the mine," Evan said quickly. "Do we go right? Left? Straight?" The split was coming up fast.

"Nope," Devlin said. "We go down."

He picked up a rock and hurled it. The rock hit a switch and the tracks shifted. Their cart dipped down a steep slope and shot around another bend. Cleo pulled on the hand brake to slow them before they flew off the tracks.

"Wow," Evan said.

"Dwarves know their way around the mines," Devlin said. "It's why the trolls force us to work."

"Force you?" Evan said. "That's terrible."

"We'd work here anyway," Devlin said. "We just don't want to work for bossy trolls."

"Speaking of trolls . . ." Cleo said.

The other cart slammed into them from behind. One of the trolls leaped into their cart and bared his yellow teeth. He growled and swung his club with the force of a sledge-hammer. Things were not looking good.

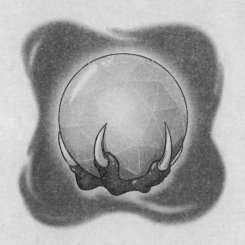

CHAPTER 8

The club smashed down. The mine cart buckled. Devlin cowered in the corner.

"Do something!" Cleo yanked the hand brake as they whipped around a curve. "You're a wizard! Use your wand!"

"I don't know how," Evan said.

"What choice do we have?"

Evan pulled out his wand, spun it in the air three times, and snapped it forward.

Orange light fired out and hit the troll in the face.

Daisies sprouted from the troll's head, and his nose started blinking like a holiday light.

The troll pounced on Evan. "I thought wizards were supposed to be mighty," he hissed.

"I thought trolls lived under bridges and ate billy goats," Evan said.

Cleo jerked on the hand brake. The troll fell forward. Evan curled his legs under the troll's chest and kicked up.

The troll lifted into the air just as the cart shot under a low bridge. His head smacked into a beam and he flew out of the cart. As he fell, they could see his blinking nose fade into darkness. A single daisy floated to the ground.

But there was no time to celebrate. *Bam!* The cart with the other troll in it slammed into them again.

Cleo climbed onto the edge of their cart and kicked the troll in the face.

The creature swung his club. It whizzed past Cleo's head and smashed the hand brake to splinters.

Devlin held up the broken handle. "I think we're in trouble!"

They whipped around another turn. The carts tipped but stayed on the track.

Cleo grabbed the handle from Devlin and stuffed it into the wheels of the troll's cart. The cart screeched and flipped over. The troll flew forward and smacked into the tunnel wall. Cleo tumbled through the air until Evan grabbed her outstretched hand and swung her back into their cart.

"That had to hurt," Cleo said, looking back.

Devlin stroked his beard. "Trolls feel no

pain," he said. "Their bones heal in minutes. They'll just be grouchy."

"They weren't grouchy before?" Cleo said.

"Grouchier," Devlin said.

The cart sped down a hill and twisted around another curve. Cold air whipped past them faster than ever.

"What do we do?" Cleo said. "We're going to be smashed to bits!"

Devlin smiled. "I told you. Dwarves know their way around the mines." He grabbed another rock and tossed it at a red lever at the side of the tunnel. The tracks swung to the left and their cart shot down a new path.

"So, Devlin," Evan said, "why were you hiding in this cart in the first place?"

"The trolls have been working us day and night. They are mining into dangerous places, areas where it is said there is great evil. It is unsafe and unwise. Now, hang on."

Devlin climbed onto the back of the cart and pressed his tiny boot against the brake. Metal squealed and sparks flew as they screeched to a halt.

They stopped on a narrow bridge made of crisscrossing timbers. Far below, trolls with glowing red eyes held torches that made creepy shadows on the walls. Dwarves carried rubble from a tunnel built of rectangular gray blocks. A huge stone dragon bared its fangs above the tunnel. Its stone claws jutted out of the walls on either side. Strange writing arched over the doorway.

Evan pulled out the Spectacles of Understanding.

"It's another poem," Evan said. "'To all

who enter. Your lives are about to end. You will be food for the worms.'"

"That's not a very good poem," Cleo said.

"It's actually quite beautiful if you read it in the original dragon language."

"Then read it to us in dragon," Devlin said.

Evan looked at the poem again. He started to hiss and growl, but gave up. "I can't make those noises without a second voice box and a forked tongue."

Suddenly, Evan grabbed his head and pulled off the glasses.

"What's the matter?" Cleo asked.

"The Spectacles of Understanding are giving me a weird headache," Evan said.

"Queen Hilliara told you not to wear them too long," Cleo said. "Now, let's climb down. We need to go in that tunnel."

Devlin cowered in the mine cart. "I'm not going in there," he said. "Dwarves might be good miners, but we're not good worm food."

"We're not going to be worm food," Evan said. "We're going to be heroes."

"That's what all worm food says before it becomes worm food."

"All right," Cleo said, lifting a leg over the edge. "Thanks for the ride, Devlin. Hope you enjoy your life in hiding."

"I'm not hiding. I'm . . . I'm . . ." Devlin frowned. "I'm coming with you."

He climbed out of the cart, and together the three friends started down the wooden bridge.

CHAPTER 9

Evan swallowed hard. Even though he was getting better at heights, they still made him queasy. Somehow, riding on Darius's back—letting someone else have control—had felt easier than climbing down this bridge. Evan went slowly. He made sure every footstep and handhold was strong.

Cleo scampered ahead, swinging between beams and supports as if she was on the school jungle gym. Evan wondered if she might be part monkey.

Devlin did all right, too. He only slowed down when he had trouble reaching a good place to grip. Dwarves were not built for climbing.

As they neared the bottom, they heard the trolls talking. Their red eyes glowed in the dim light.

"Master better know what he do, freeing the beast."

"Legend say Golden Dragon breath can melt stone."

Suddenly, the trolls stopped.

"I smell human," one said.

Evan and Cleo froze. One of the trolls looked up . . . just as Devlin jumped onto his back.

"Aaaah!" Devlin's tiny battle cry barely echoed off the walls. "I'll take you all on!"

The troll spun around, trying to shake Devlin off. But the dwarf didn't stay up there long.

Devlin yanked on the troll's ears, hopped to the ground, and ran down a side tunnel. "Bet you can't catch me!" he yelled.

The trolls chased Devlin, and Evan and Cleo climbed down.

"Do you think he'll be okay?" Evan asked.

"He'll be fine," Cleo said. "He knows these tunnels better than anyone, right?"

Evan nodded, then looked up at the stone dragon head. "Scary," he said.

"The stairway to the magical library looked scary the first time," Cleo offered.

"The stairway to the magical library *still* looks scary."

Cleo leaped onto one of the giant stone claws. "We don't have much of a choice."

"We can always—" But Cleo darted into the tunnel.

Before he followed, Evan heard a muffled cough behind him. He glanced back but saw no one.

The tunnel widened to a huge cavern filled with piles of gold. Vixa stood in the center holding the Dragon's Orb. Her eyes were glazed and her headband pulsed bright red. A huge dragon with shimmering golden scales stood before her.

"Awaken from your sleep," Vixa commanded. The Dragon's Orb glowed brightly. "You will destroy anyone who stands in Tannis's way!"

"It's the Golden Dragon," Cleo whispered.

"Oh, I thought it was the purple dragon," Evan said.

"We've got to get that orb," Cleo said. She disappeared into the shadows.

Evan began to worry. How could they face a full-grown dragon? From the look of this dragon, he didn't even want to face a baby one. He hid behind a low wall and dug in his bag. The labels on his potions and scrolls were written in a strange language.

Wait. He knew what to do! He put on his Spectacles of Understanding.

Suddenly, everything made sense! He had a potion called Slippery Slime, a bag of sneezing powder, and three scrolls. The first was a spell called Force of Mind. The second was called Meteor Impact. The third was Monstrous Transformation. He grabbed the

Force of Mind scroll and read it softly. Blue sparks appeared and started floating above Evan's hand.

Vixa and the Golden Dragon looked up.

"Fool!" Vixa bellowed. "You can't beat the greatest force this land has ever known!"

"I have to try." Evan hurled the sparks at her.

Vixa tried to dodge them, but one spark hit her sword and lifted it into the air. She bobbled the Dragon's Orb, but somehow held on. With a swipe of his hand, Evan made her sword clatter into the darkness.

"Destroy him!" Vixa commanded.

The Golden Dragon sucked in a huge breath and stepped forward. Its talons clicked on the stone floor. It was the same sound Ms. Crowley's pointy heels made on the library tile. The dragon opened its jaws and let loose a fiery breath.

Evan dove aside just before the flames struck. The heat baked his shoulders.

"It's only a matter of time before we roast you!" Vixa said.

Another flame spewed from the dragon's throat. This time, Evan sprang the other way and hid behind a chest overflowing with gold. The flame struck the treasure and melted it instantly. Evan rolled away and crept behind a statue of an ancient king.

"You can't hide forever," Vixa taunted.

"I'm good at hiding," Evan said.

"And where's your foolish partner?" Vixa said. "Did she finally become manticore food?"

"I'm right here!" Cleo said, leaping from the shadows. She cartwheeled into a back handspring and kicked Vixa in the chest.

Vixa stumbled but did not lose her grip on the Dragon's Orb. The gem on her headband

pulsed. She glared at Cleo, then turned to the mighty beast. "Destroy her!"

The Golden Dragon's tail whipped around and hit Cleo.

Evan threw his Slippery Slime potion. The bottle smashed. Green liquid spread around Vixa's feet. Soon she was sliding all over the mountain of gold, until she fell in a heap next to Cleo.

The dragon bared its fangs and lowered its head. Cleo twisted and tried to climb past Vixa, but she slipped in the slime, too.

"Nice one, Evan," Cleo cried out.

"It's the only thing I could think of!" he said.

As Cleo and Vixa struggled, Cleo's elbow hit Vixa's head. Her headband flew off and landed on the ground. The glowing stone turned dark.

Vixa shook her head. The hazy look in her eyes cleared.

"Where . . . where am I?"

"We're about to get eaten by the Golden Dragon!" Cleo said as she tried to crawl away.

Vixa lifted the glowing orb. "Halt, dragon!"

The dragon stopped and stared.

Vixa turned to Cleo and Evan. "We need to stop Tannis."

"You're Tannis's servant," Evan said. "We need to stop you!"

"I'm loyal to my father, King Ledipus."

"But you've been helping Tannis all along!" Cleo said.

"Tannis used the dark magic in this red crystal to control me." Vixa stomped on the headband. The gem made a fizzling sound. "He wants to rule the world!"

Suddenly, two creatures leaped from the shadows. They were dressed in rags and smelled like sweaty feet.

"Grim and Groo!" Evan yelled.

"Me get orb," Groo said.

"No, me get orb, dummy!" Grim said. "You have crystal!"

Grim snatched the Dragon's Orb from Vixa while Groo smashed a crystal on the floor. A magic doorway opened and the trolls dove through. As quickly as it appeared, the door vanished.

"Now what do we do?" Evan said.

"We get eaten!" Cleo said, turning to face the dragon.

"I don't think we do," Evan said.

But the Golden Dragon loomed over them . . . and it looked angry.

CHAPTER 10

"Get your sword," the dragon said to Vixa. Its voice was deep and scratchy, but for some reason it reminded Evan of home. "We have work to do."

"What sort of work?" Evan said.

"For years, the City of Bissel has protected my lair. For years, the wood elves have kept the Dragon's Orb safe. It was a balance that kept the peace. Tannis has upset this balance. He must be stopped."

Vixa ran for her sword and the dragon hunched close to Evan and Cleo.

"You two are doing a great job," the dragon said.

"Ms. Crowley?" Cleo asked, narrowing her eyes.

"Of course it's me," the dragon said. "Have you found my sister?"

"She's queen of the wood elves," Evan said. "She's got a great role."

"Excellent," the dragon said.

"Ms. Crowley, how did you end up down here?" Cleo asked.

"We never control what characters we play in these stories," the dragon said. "You two are lucky—always the heroes."

Evan smiled. Back home, he never felt like a hero. He went to school, did his homework, practiced trombone—his ho-hum life was pleasantly boring. But in all the books they'd traveled to, he was the one who saved the day.

"What do we do?" Cleo asked. "The armies are lined up on the battlefield."

Vixa returned and sheathed her sword. "Tannis told me the dragon would know a way out."

"Of course I do. It's just been a thousand years. Give me a minute."

Ms. Crowley began sniffing around. She climbed over piles of gold coins and rare gems.

Cleo picked up a handful of the treasure and let it fall through her fingers. "Too bad we can't take it with us."

"If we defeat Tannis, my father will reward you well," Vixa said.

But even if the king gave them a mountain of gold, they couldn't take it with them. All they could take home was the key to the next book. Evan figured saving Ms. Hilliard would be reward enough.

"Over here," the dragon said. "I smell fresh air behind this wall."

Cleo pushed on the stone. "It must be three feet thick," she said.

"But the breath of the Golden Dragon can melt solid stone," Evan said.

"Of course," Ms. Crowley huffed. She spread her wings, opened her jaws, and blew as hard as she could.

Only a gust of air puffed out.

"Ugh, smells like a wet fireplace!" Cleo said.

Ms. Crowley blew again.

Nothing happened.

"I must be rusty," the dragon said.

Vixa looked worried. "The fate of the kingdom rests on our shoulders."

"I've got an idea." Evan pulled out a small pouch. "Everyone stand back."

Cleo, Vixa, and the Golden Dragon backed away.

"Not you, Ms. Cr— I mean, not you, oh mighty dragon."

The dragon smiled. "No one's ever called me mighty before," she said.

"Soon, we'll be calling you 'sneezy,'" Evan said.

"What do you mean?"

"Just turn your head toward the wall."

Evan untied the pouch and tossed the sparkling dust inside into the air. It floated around Ms. Crowley's head and settled on her glimmering snout.

The dragon sucked in a breath. Then another. And another.

Evan ran for cover. "Fire in the hole!" he screamed.

"Why are we hiding behind a rock?" Cleo asked. "The dragon's breath can melt through stone!"

"Can you think of a better place?" Evan said.

"My basement," Cleo said. "I want out of this crazy world!"

When the sneezing stopped and they crawled out from behind the boulder, they found the Golden Dragon standing in front of a smooth tunnel.

"Wide enough to fly out," Ms. Crowley said. She hunched down. "Climb on."

Achoooooo!

The light was blinding.

Achooooooo!

The sound was deafening.

Achoooooo!

The heat was blazing.

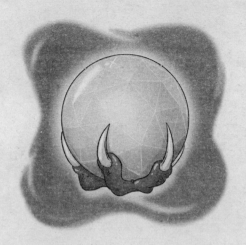

CHAPTER 11

Evan, Cleo, and Vixa burst from a hidden cave on the back of the Golden Dragon. With every pump of her great wings, they pushed faster through the air. They swooped around a mountain, through some clouds, and toward the battlefield.

"This is amazing!" Evan screamed.

"I am so tired of riding on other creatures!" Cleo screamed back.

In the distance, they saw the two armies. Arrows flew. Swords clashed. Even from far away, they could see that Tannis's army of trolls was more powerful than Queen Hilliara's forces. The trolls swarmed across the battlefield, pushing the elves and their allies back.

"We must hurry!" Vixa said.

The Golden Dragon dove. She sucked in a deep breath and breathed as hard as she could. Nothing came out. "Do you have any more sneezing powder?" she asked.

"I used it all!" Evan said.

The dragon landed on the battlefield alongside Queen Hilliara, who sat proudly atop her unicorn and carried a powerful wooden bow. The queen fired three arrows at once. Each arrow hit a different troll. All three dropped to the ground, but got back up and kept coming.

"These trolls are hard to stop!" she said.

The dragon winked and swung her tail, knocking a few trolls off a rocky ridge.

Just then, Tannis rode forward on a monstrous-looking horse. Smoke puffed from its nostrils.

"I see you've broken my enchantments," Tannis said to Vixa.

"Your magic is weak," she replied. "My father will also be free soon."

"King Ledipus is king no more. I will conquer this land and rule it all!" Tannis held up the Dragon's Orb, and the Golden Dragon bucked the kids off her back.

Ms. Crowley tried to resist, but the magic of the Dragon's Orb was too strong.

"I'm . . . I'm sorry," she said. She gnashed her teeth at Evan and Cleo.

"This is bad," Cleo said, dodging a razor-sharp claw.

"Surrender and I will spare you," Tannis said.

"We will never bow to evil!" Queen Hilliara said.

Tannis laughed. "Then you will fall to it."

A roar sounded in the distance. Several more followed, then a volley of spikes hit the ground around them. Tannis's horse backed away.

"Attack!" a familiar voice hollered.

Dozens of manticores swarmed overhead. They landed, forming a protective ring around Queen Hilliara and the kids.

"Darius!" Evan said. "You've come to help!"

"I told you manticores do not forgive easily," Darius said.

"It's been centuries since the manticores have helped Bissel," Vixa said.

"A few manticores won't stop me." Tannis held the Dragon's Orb high, and the Golden Dragon let out a threatening screech.

Darius and the manticores sprang at her, and they met the dragon in midair. Wings pounded as the fighters tumbled through the sky. The manticores clawed and bit and let their spikes fly. The dragon swung her tail like a club.

Tannis eyed Queen Hilliara. "It's time to end this." He turned to the Golden Dragon. The orb glowed. "Destroy them all!"

But then a rock hit Tannis on the side of the head.

It was Devlin, riding on the back of a hairy

boar! He aimed his slingshot and fired another stone.

"How cute," Tannis said. "Another little creature to defeat."

"Not if my friends have anything to say about it!" Devlin said.

On the top of a ridge, hundreds of dwarves lined up. They lifted their slingshots and pelted the trolls, who shrank back with fear.

"Stones," Tannis said. "Only a mere annoyance."

Evan put on his Spectacles of Understanding. He pulled out the Meteor Impact scroll and read it aloud.

"How about these stones?" Evan asked. The skies darkened and thunder crashed. Fiery stones rained from the sky.

Evan looked for Cleo, but she was nowhere to be seen. He hoped she was somewhere safe.

The trolls backed away as the dwarves charged down the hill. The dragon and manticores clashed in the stormy skies.

Dozens of flaming meteors fell to the earth. The ground shook, and Tannis's horse stumbled.

Queen Hilliara's battle cry sent the wood elves leaping from behind boulders and trees, and soon the battle raged again. For a moment it looked like the elves might stand a chance.

Cleo darted from the shadows and sprang onto the back of Tannis's horse. She spun like an Olympic gymnast, knocking the Dragon's Orb to the ground.

"No!" Tannis screamed.

Evan pulled out his last scroll and read it. He wasn't sure what the Monstrous Transformation spell did, but he figured it might be his only chance to help.

His muscles rippled and the world started shrinking around him. Wait, the world wasn't shrinking. He was getting larger! Evan grew until he was twenty, thirty, forty feet tall. He stomped forward and smashed down on the Dragon's Orb. White light burst out as the sorcerer's magic fizzled.

The Golden Dragon stopped battling the manticores. The red glow of the trolls' eyes faded to black and they all stopped fighting. Even Tannis's horse seemed to snap out of a spell. It bucked and sent Tannis tumbling to the ground.

Evan felt the magic of the scroll leave him as he took off the Spectacles of Understanding and shrank back to normal size.

A trumpet sounded, and a warrior in sparkling armor charged across the battlefield

atop a great warhorse. He wore a gleaming crown. Soldiers carrying banners of the Kingdom of Bissel galloped on either side.

"Father!" Vixa cried.

She kneeled and bowed her head as the king took his place beside her.

CHAPTER 12

King Ledipus dismounted and strode to his daughter. He was no longer pale. His hair had turned from gray to a rich brown.

"Stand, my darling," he said.

Vixa stood up, tears in her eyes. "Father, this is all my fault."

"We all fell victim to Tannis's charms," the king said, pulling a silver headband from beneath his cloak. He snapped it in two. "We must put that behind us and work to build our future."

King Ledipus turned to face the fighters. "Today we start a new chapter in our world, one where all creatures—humans, elves, manticores, dwarves, dragons, and even trolls—live in harmony. We will work together to build a future where all can find happiness."

A cheer rose up among the crowd. Even the trolls seemed happy.

The Golden Dragon landed near Queen Hilliara, her talons clicking on the ground. "Sandie . . ." she said.

The elf queen narrowed her eyes. "Barbara . . . ?"

Ms. Hilliard leaped off her unicorn and ran to her sister's side. They hugged as well as a wood elf and a dragon could hug.

"You cannot break me!" Tannis screamed. Without his power, he looked frail and weak. "I will return. And next time I'll be unstoppable!"

Tannis pulled a crystal from his robes and smashed it on the ground. A portal opened, and he jumped through. Two trolls dressed in rags followed him. In a flash of light, they disappeared.

"We have to catch him!" Cleo said.

"There's no way to know where he went," King Ledipus said.

"We won't rest until we find him," Vixa added.

King Ledipus walked over to Evan and Cleo. "You have done us a great service. As payment, I wish to give you lands of your own. Evan, you will be Wizard of the North. Cleo will be Rogue of the South."

Cleo's forehead crinkled. "I'm not sure I like the name 'rogue.'"

King Ledipus thought a little more. "Rapscallion?"

Cleo shook her head.

"Scoundrel? Rascal?"

Cleo wrinkled her nose.

"Well, do you have anything in mind?" the king asked.

"How about Cleo, Empress of the South, Queen of Cartwheels, Master of the Kicking Foot, Highness of Handsprings, Ruler of Ruckus—"

Darius cleared his throat. "Soon, her name will be longer than mine."

"We'll work out your title soon enough," King Ledipus said. He stooped to pick up a long, slender shard from the broken orb. It looked like a jagged key. He turned to Evan.

"You must take the heart of the Dragon's Orb, wizard. It holds great magical power."

"Queen Hilliara," Evan said, "mighty dragon. I would like to share this victory with both of you. Let's take this prize together."

Ms. Hilliard shook her head. "My place is here. King Ledipus and Princess Vixa will need my help."

"I'm going to stay, too," Ms. Crowley said. "I'm with my sister. And in this world, I hold great power and influence. What more could I ask for?"

"But you won't be able to wear your sharp, clicky high heels if you stay a dragon," Cleo said.

"There's nothing sharper or clickier than dragon talons," Ms. Crowley said.

"Plus, you'll always know where to find us," Ms. Hilliard added.

After all the dangers they'd faced, Evan hated leaving his favorite librarian. He had even grown to like Ms. Crowley. But this is where the two wanted to be. This place made them happy. Who was he to argue with that?

"We'll see you soon?" Cleo asked.

"I promise," Ms. Hilliard said.

Evan and Cleo grabbed the crystal key.

Letters burst from the key like a thousand crazy spiders. The letters tumbled in the air around them and began to spell words. The words became sentences, the sentences paragraphs. Before long, they could barely see through the letter confetti, and then everything went black.

CHAPTER 13

When Evan opened his eyes, Cleo was standing over him. They were back in the magical library under their school. The fire crackled quietly, warming Evan's feet. The crystal key sat on a table nearby.

"Did Ms. Hilliard really decide to stay behind?" he asked.

"Both Ms. Hilliard *and* Ms. Crowley," Cleo said. "Hey, what's that?"

Evan patted his shirt pocket. A purple scroll poked out. He unrolled it.

Dearest Evan and Cleo,

I've journeyed through *The Wizard's War* many times and have never seen such an exciting ending. You sure know how to make a story thrilling!

As for Tannis, we can't find him. It's as though he left our world entirely!

I've decided to make you both honorary librarians with full privileges to travel on to other books in the Lost Library. Enjoy your adventures, but be careful. As you've already discovered, no matter what book you enter, great challenges await!

Your friend and librarian,
Ms. Sandie Hilliard

Evan felt something else in his pocket. He reached in and pulled out two silver necklaces. Each had a fancy silver key hanging from it.

"I guess it's official," Cleo said, putting her necklace on. "We're Lost Librarians now."

"Lost Librarians? That's a terrible name," Evan said, putting on his own necklance. It felt warm against his chest.

"Do you have a better one, smarty pants?"

"How about . . . Key Hunters?" Evan suggested.

Cleo smiled. "I like it."

A deep laugh echoed behind them. "Key Hunters. Very cute."

Evan recognized the voice. A blond man wearing a pink sweater and tan pants strolled over. Even though he looked clean-cut, his stare felt evil. He held a large book sealed shut by a lock.

"Tannis!" Evan said. The man's crooked smile sent shivers down Evan's back.

"I'm not sure who Tannis is," he said. "My name is George Locke, your new librarian."

"You're Tannis," Cleo said. "I can smell you from here."

Mr. Locke's smile flickered. "I've never given a failing grade in library studies," he said. "But there's always a first. Now, if you don't mind, I'll take that key."

"No way," Evan said. His hand shot to the table, but the key was gone.

Two hunched creatures wearing blue overalls had swung from the library balconies and landed next to Mr. Locke. They had slightly green skin and long stringy hair. Their eyes glowed red.

"Grim and Groo . . ." Cleo whispered.

"I'd like you to meet my two library assistants, Gary and Glen," Mr. Locke said. "Now if you'll excuse me, I've got a book to explore."

Mr. Locke took the key from Gary and stuck it into his book. Letters burst from the pages, and within seconds, Mr. Locke and his servants were gone.

Evan and Cleo didn't even look at the title. They scooped up the book and Cleo turned the key.

Letters burst from the book like a thousand crazy spiders. The letters tumbled in the air around them and began to spell words. The words became sentences, the sentences paragraphs. Before long, they could barely see through the letter confetti. Then everything went black.

The Lost Library is full of exciting—and dangerous—books! And Evan and Cleo have a magical key to open one of them. Where will they end up next? Read on for a sneak peek of *The Titanic Treasure*!

CHAPTER 1

When Evan opened his eyes, Cleo was beside him. They were lying on long wooden chairs, facing a railing that looked out on the sparkling night sky. The floor rocked gently as water rushed below them. The breeze chilled their cheeks, and Evan longed for the warm, welcoming fire of the magical library he and Cleo had found under their school.

But the last thing he remembered happening in the library was terrible actually. Two trolls, Gary and Glen, had followed their master Mr. Locke out of the last book he and Cleo had traveled into. The trolls had stolen Evan and Cleo's crystal key and given it to Locke. Then Locke had jammed the key into a new book, and everyone in the library had disappeared into its pages. Evan was growing used to the magic of the library, but the fact that they were able to travel into actual books still amazed him. It frightened him too. If they didn't finish the story in a book, they'd be trapped in it forever. But Evan and Cleo knew Mr. Locke was up to no good. Whatever he had planned, they couldn't let him win.

Cleo wore a dark dress under a frilly white apron. Evan looked down at himself. He had on a crisp white shirt and vest with a black bow tie.

"Where are we?" Cleo asked.

Evan stood and looked over the railing. Black water glided by far below. "I think we're on a ship."

"I think we're in trouble," Cleo said.

Evan followed Cleo's gaze. She was looking at a life ring hanging on the wall behind them. It read "RMS Titanic."

Evan's stomach did a flip-flop. He knew a lot about the *Titanic*. He'd read a book about it just a few months earlier. The RMS *Titanic* was a British ocean liner. On its first voyage, it struck an iceberg and sank into the frigid waters of the North Atlantic. Of more than 2,200 passengers, only a few more than 700 survived.

"We've got to get off this ship," Evan said.

"We've got to get to the end of this story and find the key home before Locke does," Cleo replied. She and Evan were official Key

Hunters, and had the necklaces to prove it. The fancy silver keys that hung from chains under their outfits meant they could enter any book in their magic library. But it didn't mean they could get back out!

"The end of this story is that the *Titanic* sinks to the bottom of the Atlantic Ocean. April 15th of 1912."

"There has to be something else," Cleo said. "Just like in all the other books we've traveled into. We have to figure out what problem needs to be solved and then go ahead and solve it."

Evan knew she was right, but how could he focus on solving problems when all he wanted to do was watch out for icebergs?

MEET RANGER

A time–traveling golden retriever with search-and-rescue training . . . and a nose for danger!

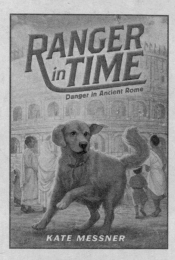